Ice Cream Cones and Heart Stones

Ice Cream Cones and Heart Stones

A Child's Grief Journey

BY CORINNE M. LITZENBERG

ILLUSTRATED BY DAPHNE A. BLAKER

RESOURCE *Publications* · Eugene, Oregon

ICE CREAM CONES AND HEART STONES
A Child's Grief Journey

Scripture taken from the Holy Bible, NEW INTERNATIONAL VERSION®, NIV® Copyright © 1973, 1978, 1984, 2011 by Biblica, Inc.® Used by permission. All rights reserved worldwide.

The five stages of the grief cycle came from the book, On Death and Dying, Elisabeth Kübler-Ross, MD, 1997, Simon and Schuster.

Resource Publications
An Imprint of Wipf and Stock Publishers
199 W. 8th Ave., Suite 3
Eugene, OR 97401

www.wipfandstock.com

PAPERBACK ISBN: 978-1-5326-9225-3
HARDCOVER ISBN: 978-1-5326-9226-0
EBOOK ISBN: 978-1-5326-9227-7

Manufactured in the U.S.A.   01/06/20

For John and Madison
In loving memory of my son, Todd —C. L. S.

For my Dad, who taught me to draw
In memory of Mitch —D. A. B.

Jeremiah 29:11 (NIV)

[11] For I know the plans I have for you," declares the LORD, "plans to prosper you and not to harm you, plans to give you hope and a future.

Madison was the first baby girl born into the family in a very long time. Her grandparents would take care of her three days a week while both of her parents went to work. She was the apple of everyone's eye, especially Granddad's. He would sing to Madison and bounce her on his knee. Baby Madison gave Granddad her first smile and first belly laugh.

When she was two, Grandma would fill up the bathtub and put Madison in with all of her tub toys. Madison smacked the water with her hands. How she loved the water! When she was three, Granddad filled up the baby pool and plopped her in with her toys. She swam on her belly and reached for the rubber duckies bobbing in the water.

"She'll be right at home at the beach house this summer," Granddad said. "Maddie the Mermaid!" he declared.

As Maddie grew older, she and Granddad grew closer. Summers at the beach were always the best times they shared together. They would hunt for sea glass along the shore. Sea glass are pieces of glass that are rounded from tumbling in the ocean. Granddad knew that after a storm and at low tide was when you could find the most sea glass.

If the sea glass piece wasn't frosted enough he would skip it back in the ocean so it could tumble longer in the salty waves. One time they found a smooth green piece shaped like a heart. "This one is a real keeper. Put it in a special place," Granddad said. Maddie put her green sea glass heart deep inside her beach bag.

Once on their beach walk when Maddie was seven, they saw lots of horseshoe crabs. Granddad and Maddie flipped over the horseshoe crabs that were on their backs, so they could swim to the ocean. Maddie found a horseshoe crab on the hot, dry sand. "This one isn't moving," she told Granddad.

Granddad said, "That's because it's dead. It didn't have any water to swim back into the sea. We did save quite a few of them. They are one of God's oldest creatures on the earth. Scientists use horseshoe crabs in their research to find cures for diseases. The red knot shorebirds depend on horseshoe crab eggs for their long journey up and down the Atlantic Ocean. It's nice to remember how important they are to us." Maddie and Granddad dug a hole and buried it in the sand. Then she drew a cross on the spot with her finger.

On the boardwalk, Granddad and Madison stopped for a treat.
They both liked butterscotch candy. They both loved vanilla ice
cream covered in chocolate syrup, and in a waffle cone.

The next day, Granddad was going to take Maddie to the lighthouse, but Granddad didn't feel well. He was coughing and felt very weak. Maddie was disappointed but she could see he wasn't himself. Maddie's dad and Grandma took Granddad to the hospital. He was in there for a few days so Maddie made him a card with the green sea glass heart taped on the front. "Make sure he gets this and give him lots of hugs and kisses from me," she told Grandma.

Later that afternoon, Maddie's dad and Grandma came home. Her dad snuggled up with her on the couch. "Where's Granddad?," she wanted to know.

Dad hugged her tight and said, "Granddad is no longer with us. He had a weak heart. The doctors and nurses did everything they could do to save him."

Maddie sobbed, "How can that be? He was going to take me to the lighthouse. I love him so much!"

Her dad answered, "We know you do. We all love him. Everything that lives also dies. Every living thing has a beginning and an end. Remember the horseshoe crabs you helped save with Granddad at the beach? And the one you could not save? Granddad told you to remember how important those horseshoe crabs are to us. Remember all of the wonderful times you have shared with him at home and at the beach. We have to hold onto all of those memories of Granddad. The memories of our loved one are a gift from God."

Maddie clenched her fist, "Why *my* Granddad?" Then she thought of Grandma, *She must miss him a whole bunch. Maybe I should give Grandma the sea glass heart.*

It was hard to sleep that night. Maddie tossed and turned and cried. Her mom heard Maddie in her bedroom. She sat next to Maddie on her bed and comforted her, "It's okay to cry, honey. It means that you deeply still love Granddad and shows how you miss him. That's what grief is all about but not everyone cries. Some people just feel very sad and hurt inside."

Her mom opened Maddie's children's Bible, "The Bible tells us that someday we will be with Jesus and Granddad will be there, too. 'For we believe that Jesus died and rose again, and so we believe that God will bring with Jesus those who have fallen asleep in him' (Thessalonians 4:14)."

Her mom read, "God's message to you is that 'He will wipe every tear from their eyes. There will be no more mourning, or crying or pain' (Revelation 21:4). No more pain for Granddad and we will see him in Heaven. The Bible promises us that. Remember that God sent His Son Jesus to suffer and die on the cross for all of us because He loves us. Jesus answered, 'I am the way and the truth and the life. No one comes to the Father except through me' (John 14:6)."

The next morning at the breakfast table Maddie asked her mom, "Can I still talk to Granddad? Can he hear me?"

Her mom replied, "Yes, you can always talk to Granddad. The beach would be a wonderful place for you to talk to God and Granddad. God is everywhere, even at the beach where you and Granddad spent so much time together."

Madison's dad explained, "Grief is like the ocean. It comes and goes in waves. There will be dark and stormy days and calm and sunny days, but slowly you will begin to heal and grow.

You can ask God to give you hope, strength, and grace to carry you through your grief journey. Then, you will start to see that there will be many more sunny days. It's important to remember that everyone's grief journey is different."

Later that week, there was a funeral service at church. There were a lot of people there. Some people Maddie did not know but they all said nice things about Granddad. Maddie sat next to Grandma. It was there she gave Grandma her precious green sea glass heart wrapped in a tissue. Grandma kissed her forehead and squeezed her tight. Maddie began to slowly understand that she would not see Granddad again alive and that he was with Jesus, in a place of peace.

As she began to grow and heal, Maddie went for her spiritual strolls on the beach to talk to Granddad and God. She would tell her Granddad what she was doing, how school was going, and about her collection of sea treasures she found each summer.

One summer day, after settling in a spot on the beach with her Grandma and her parents, Maddie went for her spiritual stroll. She walked along the hard shoreline where sandpipers were feeding and shells were gathered at the high tide line. She found silver and gold jingle shells, two moon shell caps, and a perfect scallop shell.

Maddie walked toward the ocean before heading back. She talked to her granddad and prayed for him that he was okay. She thanked God for all of her blessings, especially for her family. A wave came to her feet and when it receded, the sea foam revealed a white heart stone. Maddie stooped quickly to pick it up. She was in awe!

Part of Maddie wanted to race back to her family's beach spot and show them what she found. Another part of her just wanted to stay in that special moment. That's what she did. Then, she slowly walked back to her family praising the Lord. Maddie had a "miracle moment." She knew that Granddad and God were with her and always in her heart.

Book Talk Questions:
A Closer Look

1. What are the stages of grief in the story?

   Shock and Denial: *"How can that be? He was going to take me to the lighthouse. I love him so much."*

   Anger: *Maddie clenched her first, "Why my Granddad?"*

   Bargaining: *There is no bargaining in this story. This is when someone thinks back to a time when they could have done something differently so someone would not die. This is when someone makes "If only I would have. . ." statements.*

   *Depression and Detachmen*t: *It was hard to sleep at night. Maddie tossed and turned and cried.*

   Acceptance: *Maddie gives her Grandma the green sea glass heart. She begins to accept her loss and goes on her "spiritual strolls" to talk with her Granddad and God.*

   Note: Not everyone goes through these stages of grief and the stages can be interchangeable over time. Everyone's grief is unique and there is no time limit to a person's grief.

2. On their beach walk, Granddad and Maddie find a green sea glass heart. On Maddie's "spiritual stroll" she finds a white heart stone. What do you think is the author's meaning behind the color of the stones?

   The green sea glass heart that Granddad and Maddie found and that she gave to Grandma is a color symbol for life. The white heart stone she found is a sign of Granddad's soul in Heaven.

"Touching hearts": sea glass hearts found by the author along the shore

3. Every living thing has a life cycle. What are some other animals besides the horseshoe crab that go through stages in a life cycle?

Butterfly: egg-caterpillar-cocoon-butterfly

Human: baby-child- teenager-young adult-adult-senior citizen

4. Change is natural. How did Maddie change in the story?

Maddie was able to talk with God and Granddad on her spiritual strolls. Through her parents' suggestions on how to handle her grief and through prayer, she is able to see beyond her own grief. Maddie was able to think about her grandmother's sorrow and gave her grandmother the green sea glass heart. She began to grow and heal through her grief stages and slowly understand that Granddad was in a special place with God. She began to find her "new normal" on her grief journey.

8 Ways to Help Children Through the Loss of a Loved One

1. Help children learn to cope with losses when they are young. For a child, the death of a pet is an important loss. Talk with them about an animal's life cycle and the memories they will always have of their pet.

2. Include your children when family come to visit to share in your grief. Do not make them feel like death should not be discussed in front of them. Children will learn their response to grief from you.

3. Share pictures of the loved one you have lost and the memories you have of your loved one with children. It will help their hearts to heal.

4. Children need to discuss their feelings and fears with a close family member or close adult. Sharing their feelings will help them deal with their personal loss in a healthy way. Let them know it's okay to cry and grieve.

5. Sometimes, children need to talk to someone other than a relative. They may want to talk with a pastor, a school counselor, or a favorite teacher.

6. Remind them that everyone grieves in different ways and there is no time limit in the grief process.

7. Find ways to celebrate your loved one's loss in a special way with your child. Plant a tree or a flower garden. Read a favorite book or watch a special movie that was a favorite of your loved one.

8. Create a memory box for your child about the loved one you lost. Store movie ticket stubs, a fishing license, and other special items from your loved one. At a holiday gathering, have your child share the box of memories with other relatives. Switch out the items for the next sharing.

About the Author

Corinne has taught elementary school for thirty two years in the Diocese of Wilmington, De and Cecil County Public Schools, Md. She received her B.S. in Elementary and Special Education from The University of Delaware and her M. Ed. in Curriculum and Instruction from Loyola College of Maryland. She received her Ed.D. from  Wilmington University in Delaware where she studied environmental education. Corinne's books integrate the natural world and teach environmental activism through her characters. Her books can be found on corinnelitzenberg.com. Even in her deepest grief of losing her son, Corinne continues to live her life with purpose and meaning. Dr. Litzenberg and her husband, Dale, divide their time between the Delaware Shore and the Chesapeake Bay. They have a standard poodle named George who is a therapy dog and visits the elderly people in senior centers.

About the Illustrator

Daphne is largely self-taught in the medium of watercolor. Growing up in New Jersey, being married and raising two children there, many vacations were spent at the Jersey Shore. She and her husband Walt are retired and living near the beach in Lewes, DE, but prefer beaches with palm trees. She has produced many landscapes, florals and still lifes, and is a member of the Cape Artists, Rehoboth Art League and Delaware Watercolor Society. More of her work can be seen at watercolors-by-daphne.vpweb.com.